W9-CUO-654

SADDLEBACK
EDUCATIONAL PUBLISHING

think green

Water
Conservation

SADDLEBACK
EDUCATIONAL PUBLISHING

Three Watson
Irvine, CA 92618-2767
Website: www.sdlback.com

ISBN-13: 978-1-59905-352-3
ISBN-10: 1-59905-352-7
eBook: 978-1-60291-680-7

Printed in China

12 11 10 09 08   9 8 7 6 5 4 3 2 1

Contents

The Earth's Water

Water is one of the most essential elements for all forms of life on Earth. All plants and animals, including humans, need water to survive. Water is found almost everywhere on Earth. Almost 71% of Earth's surface is covered with water. Water is found in the form of groundwater, soil moisture, snow, ice, and surface waters. *Groundwater* is water stored in underground aquifers. *Surface water* is visible and is stored in oceans, streams, rivers, lakes, and manmade reservoirs. A large portion of water is locked in the form of ice in glaciers and polar ice caps. Water is also present in the atmosphere in the form of water vapor. Due to its abundance of water, Earth is known as "the blue planet."

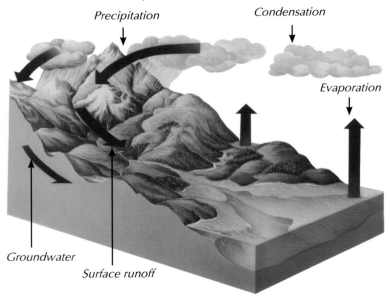

The Water Cycle

Earth has almost the same amount of water as it had millions of years ago. The water we drink today is the same water the dinosaurs drank. Water on Earth keeps moving through its various states—solid, liquid, and vapor. This continual movement of water on, above, and below the surface of Earth is known as the *water cycle or hydrologic cycle*. The water cycle helps Earth recycle water naturally, with help from the sun's heat. Though the water cycle is a continuous process, it has no starting or ending point. It is made up of several processes:

- **Evaporation**: Heat and energy from the sun warm the water of oceans, lakes, and rivers. The warm water changes from liquid into a gas called *water vapor*. Since water vapor is lighter than dry air, it rises into the atmosphere. This process is known as *evaporation*.

- **Condensation**: In the atmosphere, water vapor comes into contact with cooler air and changes into liquid. Water vapor takes the form of little water droplets in the air and forms clouds. This is called *condensation*.

- **Precipitation**: When a lot of water vapor condenses into droplets, the clouds become so heavy that air cannot hold them anymore. As a result, the droplets fall from the sky. This is called *precipitation*. Precipitation occurs on Earth in the form of rain, hail, snow, or sleet.

- **Collection**: When water falls back to Earth, it may fall on oceans, lakes, or rivers, or it may fall back onto land. On land, water seeps into the ground and becomes *groundwater*.

Oceans

Oceans are large bodies of water that cover about 71% of Earth's surface. Oceans contain about 97% of Earth's total water. The five oceans on Earth are the Pacific, Atlantic, Indian, Arctic, and Southern Oceans. The oceans are made up of smaller water bodies known as seas, bays, and gulfs.

Glaciers

Glaciers are thick layers of compacted snow and ice that flow like slow-moving rivers. The snow in glaciers accumulates over many years. Some glaciers in the Canadian Arctic icecaps are around 100,000 years old. They are the largest storage of fresh water on Earth. Around 69% of the world's total fresh water is in the form of glaciers and ice caps. Scientists worry that if these glaciers and ice caps start melting, sea levels could rise by as much as 210 feet. About 10%–11% of the world's total landmass is covered in glacial ice. Glacial ice is found all over the world except in Australia. Most glaciers are located in Greenland and Antarctica. Glaciers can range in size from as small as a football field to hundreds of miles long.

Rivers

Rivers are natural waterways flowing on the Earth's surface. Rivers carry water over land from a higher altitude to a lower altitude. When rain falls on the ground, it either seeps in or flows downhill into rivers and lakes. Rivers eventually drain their water into the seas and oceans.

Aquifer

Aquifers are underground water storage areas. Aquifers store water between layers of rocks, sand, and gravel. Aquifer water is cleaner in comparison to surface water and is also free from bacteria. Rocks and soil filter out pollutants. The water in aquifers can be pumped out by digging wells into the ground. Aquifer water is a source of fresh water that can be used for household and agricultural purposes.

Lakes and Reservoirs

Lakes are water bodies surrounded by land. Lakes form when water flows to a place that is enclosed by higher land on all sides. Most lakes are a source of fresh water, but some lakes are even saltier than the ocean. Reservoirs are manmade lakes where water is stored for future use. They form when dams are built on rivers.

Did you know?

Earth has about 326 million cubic miles of water.

Usable Water

Usable water means water that we use daily for many purposes. We use water for drinking, washing, bathing, cooking, and watering plants and food crops. Earth has plenty of water, but not all the water on Earth is usable. About 97% of Earth's water is stored in the oceans. Ocean water is salty and therefore unusable. This means that only 3% of the water on Earth is fresh water, which is usable water. Most of this fresh water, however, is locked in glaciers and ice caps, which makes it unusable. Only 1% of the water remains usable for humans. This usable water can be found in groundwater, lakes, and rivers. Americans use a large amount of water every day. An average American family of four uses about 400 gallons of water a day.

Ways We Use Water

- For agriculture
- In homes
- By industry
- To generate thermoelectric power
- For mining
- To water livestock
- In hotels and restaurants

What makes water unusable?

- Hazardous waste
- Improperly disposed of toxic products
- Improperly disposed of wastes
- Use of chemical pesticides and fertilizers
- Water contaminated with motor oil, grease, and paint

Virtual Water: Embedded Usable Water

Water is used to produce food and other goods. The largest percentage of usable water is used by agriculture and industry. The water that is embedded in our food and manufactured products is called "virtual water." For example, about 265 gallons of water is needed to produce two pounds of wheat. So the virtual water of this two pounds of wheat is 265 gallons. Virtual water is also present in dairy products, soups, beverages, and liquid medicines. Every day, humans consume and use lots of virtual water. The content of virtual water varies according to products. For instance, to produce two pounds of meat requires about 5 to 10 times as much water as to produce two pounds of bread, rice, or vegetables. In the United States, the average person consumes more than 175 cubic feet of virtual water per day from a meat-based diet.

Did you know?

About 280 cubic miles of water evaporates into the atmosphere every day.

Facts You Should Know

- About one gallon of water is used to make a quarter pound of hamburger.
- About 39,090 gallons of water is required to manufacture a new car, including its tires.
- A birch tree evaporates nearly 70 gallons of water per day.
- One inch of rainfall gives about 27,000 gallons of water per acre of land.
- About 1,500 gallons of water is needed to make just one barrel of beer.

Potable Water

Water that is safe and suitable for human consumption is known as *potable* water. Potable water does not contain salt and is also known as drinking water. Potable water is free from contaminants and other impurities that can cause diseases. Potable water is actually *treated water.* Water from streams, rivers, springs, and lakes is treated to remove impurities and make it potable. Potable water is not equally distributed throughout the world. Most of Earth's fresh water is located in North America. Each year, more than 671,000 cubic feet of water is available per person in North America. In contrast, just over 166,000 cubic feet of water is available annually for a person in Asia.

Where does potable water come from?

Potable water comes from two sources: groundwater and surface water. Groundwater is found underground in watersheds, springs, and aquifers. Surface water includes lakes, streams, and rivers. Both these water sources are dependent on rain, snowfall, and other forms of precipitation. Rain and snowfall recharge groundwater sources as well as surface water sources. About 74% of the fresh water used in the United States comes from surface water. The other 26% comes from groundwater sources. Groundwater is an important source of potable water in the arid regions. The western states of the United States get their potable water mainly from groundwater reserves.

Who is responsible for potable water quality?

Governments are responsible for providing safe potable water. Water can contain around 80 contaminants that can cause health hazards. The responsibilities of governments include:
- Checking for contaminants in water
- Testing the water system
- Distribution and supply of potable water
- Recording consumer complaints
- Taking necessary action against these complaints

Water Contaminants

Contaminants are impurities that pollute water. They are harmful for humans as well as for plants and animals. Contaminated water can cause serious diseases. At any given time, about 50% of the world's hospital beds are occupied by patients suffering from waterborne diseases. About 3,900 children die every day due to lack of potable water. Contaminants can be natural or manmade. Natural contaminants can come from soil erosion or rocks. Manmade contaminants include chemicals and toxic materials from industrial, agricultural, or household sources. Some common water contaminants:

- Antifreeze and coolants
- Batteries, new and used
- Cleaning solvents
- Disinfectants
- Explosives
- Food processing wastes
- Glues, adhesives, and resins
- Greases
- Printing and photocopying chemicals
- Laboratory chemicals
- Metal finishing solutions
- Oils (petroleum based)
- Paints, primers, thinners, dyes, stains
- Photo development chemicals
- Tanning (leather) industry chemicals

What you can do?

- Always be informed about the source of your drinking water.
- Always be informed about the surroundings of your drinking water source.
- Always be informed about the contaminants that pollute drinking water sources.
- Participate actively in your community water-conservation activities.
- Always be observant about chemical spills and leakage, and report these activities.
- Reuse oil, paints, etc. wherever possible.
- Use and dispose of chemicals properly.

World Water Day

Potable water is becoming scarce in many parts of the world. About 1.1 billion people around the world do not have access to enough safe, clean potable water. To highlight the importance of conserving water, the United Nations has declared March 22 as "World Water Day."

Did you know?

At any particular moment, the atmosphere contains about 3,100 cubic miles of water, mainly in the form of water vapor. This water could make a one-inch covering of water around our entire planet.

How Much Do We Need?

Water is important for our continued existence on Earth. We need water for our survival, to produce food crops and meet our energy requirements. Water is used in irrigation, industries, electricity production, livestock, mining, and for public consumption. According to the World Health Organization, each person requires a minimum of about five gallons of water every day. However, it is difficult to estimate the amount of water needed to maintain minimum living standards. The use of water varies greatly among people of different regions. An average American uses about 80–100 gallons of water per day, while water usage per person per day in Asia is only 22 gallons and in Africa just 12 gallons.

Agriculture

We need water to produce our food. About 70% of Earth's fresh water is used for *agriculture*. Water is used in agriculture to irrigate fields. A large amount of water is needed to cultivate crops. It takes about 1,000 tons of water to produce one ton of grain.

To produce just 2 pounds of rice, we need about 350 gallons of water. To produce just 2 pounds of wheat we need about 250 gallons of water.

Industries

Industries also need large quantities of water. Industries that produce metals, wood and paper products, chemicals, and oils are major users of water. Various industrial processes such as fabrication, processing, washing, diluting, cooling, and transportation of finished products require large amounts of water as well. Every year, industries consume about 22% of the global usable water.

Domestic Supply

Domestic use of water includes water used in households every day. Domestic use includes water for general household purposes such as drinking, cooking, bathing, washing clothes and dishes, flushing toilets, and watering lawns and gardens. Domestic use of water accounts for about 8% of the total water used in a year.

Thermoelectric Power

Thermoelectric power is the process of generating electricity from water. It is the largest consumer of water in the United States. Electricity is generated with the help of steam-driven turbine generators. Water is used in power plants to cool machines. Thermoelectric power uses 70% saline water and 30% fresh water. It consumes about 52% of the total surface water consumed and more than 1% of the total groundwater used.

Livestock

Livestock are domesticated animals raised on farms. Domesticated animals such as beef cattle, dairy cows, chickens, horses, pigs, sheep, and goats are called *livestock*. Livestock produces meat, poultry, eggs, milk, and other dairy products. A beef cow needs about 15 gallons of water per day, and a dairy cow requires about 42 gallons per day. Livestock animals consume more than 1% of the total surface water used and about 2% of the groundwater used.

Mining

Mining is the process of extracting valuable minerals from the ground. These valuable minerals include coal, oil, gold, silver, copper, and diamonds and other precious stones. The process of quarrying, milling, crushing, screening, and washing requires plenty of water. Mining consumes about 1% of the groundwater used.

Water Usage in Various Countries

In Europe, about 54% of water usage is by industries, while agriculture uses only 33%. Developing countries utilize most of their water for agriculture. For example, in Africa, about 88% of all available water is used in agriculture, while domestic supply accounts for 7% and industry for only 5%. In India, agriculture alone consumes nearly 90% of all water. The country requires only 7% of its water usage for industry and just 3% for domestic purposes.

Precious Water: Water Management

Large parts of Earth are covered in water. But most of Earth's water is saline, or salty, and thus unfit for human consumption. Only about 1% of all water is available for our use. This makes water a precious commodity. Therefore, it is essential for water to be managed properly. Water management aims to limit the amount of water usage so that fresh water can be conserved. Water management also helps to determine the location and available amounts of fresh water and to estimate the requirements of various water users.

World Water Forum

The World Water Forum is a worldwide initiative for better water management. This forum, sponsored by the World Water Council, aims to create global awareness about water and to find solutions to achieve water security. The first World Water Forum was held in 1997 in Marrakech, Morocco. Since then, every third year the World Water Council organizes the World Water Forum in collaboration with the world's countries. So far, four meetings of the World Water Forum have been held in different parts of the world. The fifth will be held in Istanbul, Turkey, in March of 2009.

The main purposes of the forum:
- To highlight the importance of water
- To create awareness about water issues
- To formulate concrete proposals
- To generate government intervention where needed

Water Management Policy

The world's population is rising steadily, which will create further water shortages in many places. The scarcity of water is already a concern in many areas. To manage water better, governments have formulated many policies to conserve water. These policies, known as *water management policies*, aim to:

- Find new areas where usable water is available
- Find areas with scarce water
- Supply water to water-scarce areas
- Ensure proper use of available water
- Make people aware of water wastage
- Save money by saving water
- Save electricity by saving water
- Find solutions for growing water needs
- Maintain quality of surface water and groundwater
- Protect water from getting contaminated

Water Recycling

Water recycling is a process of reusing water. Wastewater comes from many household and industrial sources, and most types of wastewater can be recycled. Some wastewater can be recycled directly. Other types of wastewater can be recycled by water treatment plants. Treated wastewater is nonpotable water and is used to irrigate fields, flush toilets, and in industries and landscape irrigation.

Water Management Techniques

Water management techniques broadly cover three areas: reducing water loss or saving water, increasing awareness among people, and reusing wastewater. Some of these techniques:

- Harvest rainwater
- Apply xeriscaping (land use planning) to reduce water wastage
- Install new and efficient sanitary equipment
- Use measuring equipment to determine water usage
- Reuse water used for sterilizing equipment
- Store and reuse the condensate water released by air conditioners
- Reuse water used for cooling machines in industry

Benefits of Water Management

- Saves precious water
- Preserves water quality
- Saves wildlife
- Reduces possibility of floods
- Improves living conditions for aquatic animals

Did you know?

If all the water on Earth were poured onto the United States, it would form a 90-mile-deep layer of water.

Water Shortage:
Population Growth

On October 12, 1999, there were 6 billion people living on Earth. Each year, 80 million more people are added to the world's population. The ever-increasing population means an increased demand for fresh water. About 60% of the world's population lives in Asia, but the fresh water available there is only about 30% of world supplies. To meet this shortage, Asia needs an extra 84 billion cubic yards of water each year. This is equal to the entire annual flow of the Rhine River in Europe.

Factors Affecting Water Shortage

- Population growth
- Food production
- Rising temperatures
- Climate change
- Water quality
- Water demand
- Water shortage
- Immigration
- Poverty
- Urbanization

Urbanization

Urbanization is the migration of people from villages to towns and cities. People migrate to urban areas in search of new opportunities. Urbanization leads to a greater concentration of people in cities. The United Nations has predicted that 19 out of the 25 big cities in the developing world will become overpopulated by 2025. This will create severe scarcity of water in these cities. The United Nations made serious attempts to curb this crisis through an initiative called Millennium Development Goals. One of its important objectives is to reduce the amount of population without safe drinking water and sanitation by 50% by 2015.

Climate Change

Climate change is the variation in a region's climate due to global warming. Earth is getting warmer, which causes melting of glaciers, increased droughts in some areas, and increased precipitation in others. All these factors greatly affect water availability. Studies have shown that about three billion people will suffer from water shortage in the near future.

Immigration and Water Supply

Immigration is migrating from one's native land and settling in a new country. Humans migrate to other places according to their comfort and needs. Immigration increases the population of a country, which creates water shortages. It is estimated that 1 million people migrate every year to the United States. By 2050, this figure will go up to about 10 million. Scientists predict that about 2 billion people could face water shortages by 2050.

Population Growth in Asia

The population of India, China, and Pakistan will increase by about a billion people by 2050. By 2050, India is projected to add 519 million people, China 211 million, and Pakistan nearly 200 million.

Water Shortage: Drought

Drought is a natural phenomenon. It is usually a long period of dry weather, which causes a serious shortage of water. Drought occurs due to lack of rainfall, which causes adverse effects on the plants, animals, and human beings of a particular region. During droughts, there is very little moisture in the air. This causes breathlessness, dryness, and thirst. Drought may last a few months, or it may occur for several years. Drought threatens food production, hinders economic development, and damages ecosystems.

Deadly Droughts

The effects of drought can be even more severe than other natural calamities. The 1988 U.S. drought caused a loss of about $40 billion, which exceeded the loss caused by Hurricane Andrew in 1992, the Mississippi River floods of 1993, and the San Francisco earthquake in 1989. The 1984–85 droughts in the horn of Africa led to a famine that killed about 750,000 people.

Causes of Drought

- Irregular pattern of rainfall or snow over different areas
- Changing pattern of rainfall or snow in an area over a period of years
- Water supplies are not sufficient to meet the requirements
- Changing pattern of blowing winds
- Change of ocean currents

Adverse Effects of Drought

- Soil erosion
- Loss of vegetation
- Infestations of destructive insects and other pests
- Survival of rare animals and plants endangered
- Wildfires
- Dust storms
- Loss of crops and livestock
- Migration of humans, animals, and birds
- Problem of public health and safety
- Loss of swampland, rivers, and lakes

Three Types of Drought

1. *Meteorological drought* occurs due to low rainfall.
2. *Hydrological drought* occurs due to shrinking water levels.
3. *Agricultural drought* occurs due to less moisture in air and soil.

Meteorological Drought

Meteorological drought occurs when rainfall decreases over a period of time. Diminished rainfall leads to a reduction in soil moisture, and this affects vegetation. The definition of what constitutes a drought varies greatly by region, because some regions normally get much less rain than others. For example, the average annual rainfall in the U.S. Southwest is much less than that in the Northwest.

Hydrological Drought

Hydrological drought is the result of decreased rainfall and its effects on water levels. As rainfall decreases, the water levels in rivers, reservoirs, lakes, and aquifers also decreases proportionately. Usually hydrological droughts occur after meteorological droughts. They affect ecosystems, hydroelectrical power production, and water usage of commercial, recreational, industrial, and urban facilities.

Agricultural Drought

Agricultural drought is the result of decreased rainfall and its effects on crops. Dry air and reduced moisture in soil affect crops drastically. As the water levels in rivers, reservoirs, lakes, and aquifers decreases, this affects irrigational facilities. Apart from low rainfall, water wastage is also an important reason for agricultural droughts. Usually these occur after meteorological and hydrological droughts.

Some Major Droughts of the World

- **Drought of Sahel**
  The prolonged drought of Sahel in the early 1980s and 1990s is considered one of the most destructive droughts ever. Sahel is a semi-arid region of the Sahara Desert in Africa. This drought affected around 150 million people in 20 countries and caused 100,000 to 250,000 deaths.
- **The 1876 Drought of China**
  The most destructive drought in China occurred between 1876 and 1879. Wetlands, lakes, and rivers turned dry and affected crops and livestock. Lack of food spread in nine provinces in an area covering 390,000 square miles. An estimated death toll of nine million people was recorded.

Did you know?

Nine of the world's countries possess 60% of Earth's available fresh water supply. They are Brazil, Russia, China, Canada, Indonesia, the United States, India, Colombia, and the Democratic Republic of Congo.

Water Shortage:
Water Prices Increasing

Water is now a precious commodity. The shortage of water and increasing demand for it worldwide are the main reasons for the rise in water prices. In recent years, excessive consumption of water in households has led to water utility companies raising their prices. The price of clean water will likely continue to climb.

Determining Water Prices

In the United States, water prices have increased by about 27%. The price people pay for water is determined largely by three factors: (1) the cost of transporting it from its source to the consumer, (2) total demand for the water, and (3) price subsidies. Treatment of water to remove contaminants also can add to the rising cost of water.

Reasons for Increased Water Prices

- Growing populations
- Inefficient irrigation
- Pollution
- Rapid industrial development
- Inefficient and insufficient water resources
- Climatic change
- Inefficient water management

Population

Water is a limited resource, whereas population is growing at a faster rate than ever before. Increasing population means increasing demand for water. As the population grows, the demand for water also increases, but the amount of water available to each person is less and less.

Climatic Changes

Climatic changes happen partly because heat from the sun melts ice, adding more water to the oceans. The fresh water from the ice, mixed with ocean water, becomes saltwater, which cannot be used as drinking water. Temperature rises result in icebergs melting, but iceberg water is of no use once it becomes saltwater.

Did you know?

In the last five years, water prices have increased by about 32% in the United Kingdom, 45% in Australia, 50% in South Africa, and 58% in Canada.

Water Demand

Water is required for survival by everyone on Earth. As the population increases more and more quickly, the demand for water also grows. People require a lot of water to fulfill their needs. In drought regions, they have to conserve water because they do not have enough money for underground water pipes. Wells are their only source of water. Farmers need water for irrigating their crops. As the demand increases, water shortages occur.

Facts About the Global Water Crisis

- Water-related diseases are one of the leading causes of disease and death in the world.
- About 88% of all diseases are caused by unsafe drinking water, improper sanitation, and poor hygiene.
- Nearly 50% of the water supply projects in the developing world fail.

Water Wasters

People waste water both indoors and out. Wasting water resources harms the Earth. Water is the most important resource, required for most things we do. We waste water everyday while cleaning, cooking, and drinking. Water wastage also results in rising costs for other things, such as electricity. By saving water, we can also save money. Installing efficient taps and flush systems goes a long way in saving money and water. Leakage can cause water wastage. Check for leaks both inside and outside the house and repair them immediately.

Water Wasters

- Showers (2-5 gallons per minute)
- Bathroom Sinks (2-5 gallons per minute)
- Toilet (2-5 gallons per flush)
- Dishwasher (25 gallons per load)
- Kitchen Sink (2-5 gallons per minute)
- Washing Machine (30 gallons per load)

Water Wasted In One Month From Leaks

Source	Gallons Wasted Per Month
A slow steady drip	(100 drops per minute) 350 gallons
A fast drip	about 600 gallons
A small stream	2,000-2,700 gallons
A large stream	4,600 gallons

Water Use Statistics

Indoor water use in the typical single family home is 69.3 gallons in the United States.

Use	Gallons per Capita	Percentage of Total Daily Use
Showers	11.6	16.8%
Clothes Washers	15.0	21.7%
Dishwashers	1.0	1.4%
Toilets	18.5	26.7%
Baths	1.2	1.7%
Leaks	9.5	13.7%
Faucets	10.9	15.7%
Other Domestic Uses	1.6	2.3%

Installing efficient water systems and regularly checking of leaks can reduce the daily household water use by about 35 percent to about 45.2 gallons every day.

Use	Gallons per Capita	Percentage of Total Daily Use
Showers	8.8	19.5%
Clothes Washers	10.0	22.1%
Dishwashers	0.7	1.5%
Toilets	8.2	18.0%
Baths	1.2	2.7%
Leaks	4.0	8.8%
Faucets	10.8	23.9%
Other Domestic Uses	1.6	3.5%

Did you know?

Since 1960, use of water for irrigation has increased by more than 60%.

Water-Saving Etiquette

Saving water is essential for the survival of humans on Earth. People need water for various purposes, from drinking to cleaning. In the United States, the total amount of water used by households is about 408 billion gallons a day. Americans usually use most of the water for flushing toilets and bathing, followed by laundry, cleaning dishes, cooking, and drinking.

Ways to Reduce Outdoor Water Wastage

- Avoid overwatering lawns and gardens.
- Water lawns and gardens early in the morning to reduce evaporation.
- Don't water lawns or gardens when rain is expected.
- Use a layer of mulch around plants, which reduces evaporation.
- Don't water sidewalks or driveways.
- Regularly check for leaks and repair them.
- Do not sprinkle unnecessarily.
- Use a timer on sprinklers.

Ways to Reduce Water Wastage Inside Homes

- Install faucet aerators.
- Regularly check for leaks.
- Do not run tap unnecessarily.
- Turn off tap while brushing teeth and shaving.
- Install an energy-efficient hot-water system.
- Conserve water and reuse when possible.
- When cleaning dishes by hand, it is better to fill a bowl or sink.
- Use dishwasher only when fully loaded.
- Purchase dishwashers that save energy and conserve water.

Did you know?

An average person unknowingly wastes about 30 gallons of water per day.

Conserving Water When Washing Vehicles

- Wash the vehicle on grass instead of on pavement or sidewalks.
- Give the vehicle a sponge bath.
- Use soapy water to wash the vehicle.
- Use a bucket of soapy water for washing the vehicle instead of running water.
- Clean your vehicle with a hose that has an automatic shutoff nozzle.

Recycle Water

Most of the water used in homes can be recycled. Toilet water cannot be used again, but other wastewater can be. Wastewater that can be reused can be collected from different sources. The main sources of wastewater collection in a home:

- Washing machine
- Bathtub
- Shower
- Utility sink
- Bathroom sink
- Dishwasher
- Kitchen sink

Water-Saving Ideas

- Install faucet aerators.
- Take shorter showers.
- Choose plants that require less water.
- Use low-flow showerheads.
- Recycle water.
- Do not run water unnecessarily.
- Do not run tap while scrubbing dishes and pots.
- Use brooms instead of hose for cleaning sidewalks and driveways.
- Install new toilets that use less water per flush.
- Use a shutoff nozzle on tap.
- Reuse wastewater to irrigate plants.
- Store drinking water in the refrigerator.
- Avoid running water to defrost frozen foods such as vegetables and fruits.
- Start a compost pile instead of putting food scraps in the garbage disposal.
- Install an instant water heater.
- Water the lawns and gardens early in the morning
- Plant native and drought-resistant grasses, shrubs, trees, and plants.
- Do not buy toys, such as squirt guns, that require water.

Saving Water in the Bathroom

The *bathroom* is a room that usually has a bathtub, shower, sink, and toilet. The largest amount of indoor water use occurs in the bathroom, with 41% used for toilet flushing and 33% used for bathing. In the United States, water used together in baths, showers, toilets, and sinks accounts for about 75% of the total indoor water use. About 30% of this water is used in showers and about 27% in toilets.

Why is it important to save water in the bathroom?

Water is one of the most important resources on Earth. We cannot live without it. Wasting water means inviting a water crisis in the future. We should save water for the future of our planet. By saving water, we can save on our energy bills. There are many ways to save water in the bathroom, such as installing low-flow showerheads and not letting the water run while brushing and shaving. We can save more than 10,000 gallons of water by reducing two minutes of shower time. Always check for leaks in toilets, because leaks account for about 10, 000 gallons of wasted water every year.

Dos and Don'ts

- Install water-saving devices.
- Install a low-flow showerhead.
- Take shorter showers.
- Fill the tub while taking a bath.
- Run water only when needed.
- Install an ultra-low-flush toilet.
- Don't flush toilet unnecessarily.
- Don't let the water run if not necessary.
- Take showers instead of baths.
- Don't overfill your bathtub.
- Don't use the toilet to dispose of paper towels, diapers, etc.

Did you know?

If every American used a gallon of water less every day, we would conserve the same amount of water taken every two days from the Great Lakes.

Good Water-Conserving Habits

- Recycle and save water.
- Always check for leaks in toilets.
- Insulate hot-water pipes.
- Take shorter showers.
- Turn off water while brushing and shaving.
- Avoid running water while shampooing or soaping.
- Bathe small children together.

Saving Water in the Kitchen

The *kitchen* is a place in a home used for cooking and preparing food. Kitchens contain cooking devices, washing equipment, and a sink for cleaning utensils, fruits, and vegetables. Large amounts of water are used in the average kitchen, amounting to about 15% of household water.

Saving Water While Cooking

- Use less water for cooking.
- Always cover pans or pots while cooking.
- Use leftover cooking water for soups or sauces.
- Defrost frozen vegetables and fruits in the refrigerator. Don't wash them under a running tap.

Saving Water While Washing Dishes

- Run the dishwasher only when it is fully loaded.
- When washing dishes by hand, fill the sink or a bowl instead of using running water.
- Soak pans or bowls instead of scrubbing them under running water.

Did you know?

About 25 gallons of water can be saved by using a filled sink or bowl rather than running water from a faucet.

Good Water-Conserving Habits

- Install flow-controlled aerators on taps.
- Insulate hot-water pipes.
- Do not use the sink for garbage disposal. Use the garbage can.
- Try to wash dishes by hand instead of using a dishwasher.
- Always turn taps off tightly.
- Install fit spray taps.
- Reuse clean household water, such as water used to boil vegetables or eggs.

Dos and Don'ts

- Check for leaks and repair them.
- Wash vegetables and fruits in a filled sink or basin rather than under a running tap.
- Keep the lid over a pan while boiling vegetables.
- Never leave a running tap while cleaning vegetables or fruits.
- Minimize the number of cooking utensils and dishes used.

Saving Water in the Garden

A garden is a piece of land where flowers, fruits, vegetables, and other plants are grown. On average, 50% to 70% of home water is used outdoors for watering lawns and gardens. Saving water in the garden saves money by reducing water bills. It could also help in maintaining a healthy garden.

Why is it important to save water in the garden?

Saving water in the garden will save about 750 to 1,500 galloons of water every month. Watering plants early in the morning prevents the growth of fungus. It also helps in preventing water loss by reducing evaporation. Using a layer of mulch around plants helps in reducing evaporation, which could save hundreds of gallons of water every year. Saving water in the garden helps reduce water bills.

Good Water-Conservation Habits

- Install a drip irrigation system.
- Use homemade compost for your plants.
- Group plants according to their watering needs.
- Water the garden only when needed.
- Install a water-recycling system in your garden.

Dos and Don'ts

- Water the roots and soil rather than spraying water in the leaves and stems.
- Regularly check garden taps and pipes for leaks, and repair them immediately.
- Do not water the garden during windy days, as the wind will blow the water to where it is not required.
- Choose plants that are native to your local climate.
- Use a water-efficient nozzle for your hose that ranges from high to low spray.
- Do not overwater the garden.
- Install a tap timer for watering the plants.
- Choose drought-resistant plants for your garden.
- Use a watering can rather than a hose.

Use Graywater in the Garden

Graywater is water that has been used in the home. This water includes wastewater from sinks, showers, laundry, and kitchen. Graywater does not include water from toilets. It often contains soaps, detergents, and fats. Graywater can be used in gardens during droughts or when there is a shortage of water. Dish, shower, sink, and laundry water accounts for about 50% to 60% of wastewater that can be reused. Graywater can be used in the garden in the following ways:

- Add graywater directly to the soil instead of using a sprinkler.
- Do not use graywater for seedlings or young plants.
- Use graywater on larger areas, and also spray fresh water, which helps in preventing an increase of sodium salts.
- Water only the hardier plants with graywater.
- Use graywater only when it is cool.
- Do not apply graywater directly to foliage; use on roots and surrounding soil.
- Nonedible plants can be watered with graywater from baths and showers.

Drought-Resistant Plants

Drought-resistant plants can be planted in your garden to save water. Some common drought-resistant plants:

- Eucalyptus
- Pines
- Poppy
- Tulip
- Juniper
- Lavender
- Marigolds

Crops That Require Little Water

- Turnips
- Parsnips
- Beets
- Onions
- Carrots
- Rhubarb
- Asparagus

Benefits of Saving Water in the Garden

- Saves money by reducing water bills
- Reduces maintenance time
- Protects the environment
- Healthy and beautiful garden
- Water can be reused and recycled

Did you know?

Watering the garden with a sprinkler wastes a lot of water. A sprinkler running for two hours can use about 500 gallons of water.

Saving Water on the Lawn

A *lawn* is an area planted with grass outside a house. Generally, a lawn is part of a garden planted near a home. Maintaining a green lawn requires a large amount of water. About 32% of residential outdoor water is used in caring for lawns. For a healthy lawn, it is necessary to have proper watering techniques. Proper watering not only helps to build a healthier lawn but also helps in saving water. Lawns are very popular in the United States, with approximately 32 million acres of lawn.

Lawns Help the Environment

Lawns are beneficial for the environment as well as for human health. They act as filters and help to clean the environment by absorbing pollutants. Each year, lawns trap nearly 12 million tons of dust and dirt released into the atmosphere over the United States. Lawns also help purify water entering the ground. The microbes in a lawn's roots and soil act as a filter to capture many types of pollutants. A healthy lawn absorbs six times more rainfall than a wheat field and four times more than a hay field. An average-sized lawn can give about nine tons of air conditioning effect, which is higher than the central air conditioning in many homes

Tips for Saving Water in the Lawn

- Water the lawn only when necessary.
- Avoid shallow watering of the lawn.
- Position the sprinkler so water can easily disperse to every area.
- Trim the grass at a higher than normal level. It could help in conserving water.
- Avoid watering the lawn when rain is expected.
- Remove living or dead organic matter (thatch) from the lawn.
- Group plants that need the same amount of water.
- Use a rain gauge for measuring the level of water.

Dos and Don'ts

- Avoid overwatering the lawn.
- Check for sprinkler or hose leaks and repair them.
- Do not overfertilize the lawn.
- Avoid watering the lawn in the afternoon.
- Try to water lawns in early morning, which helps reduce evaporation.
- Choose native plants, grass, trees, or shrubs for your lawn.
- Do not run the sprinkler or hose unnecessarily.
- Don't cut the lawn too short.
- Use a sprinkler timer.
- Use sprinklers that disperse large drops of water.
- Avoid watering the lawn daily.
- Use drip irrigation.
- Use mulch around plants, trees, and shrubs.

Did you know?

Placing lawn sprinklers properly could help save about 500 to 1,500 gallons of water every month.

Xeriscaping

Xeriscaping is a form of landscaping that helps conserve water. The term *xeriscape* is derived from the Greek words *xeros*, which means "dry," and *scape*, which means "a type of view or scene." Xeriscaping was developed in Colorado in 1981. It uses landscaping that requires only a small amount of water. It is also an eco-friendly form of landscaping that uses different varieties of indigenous and drought-tolerant plants. Xeriscaping uses minimal fertilizer and pesticides, both of which can cause damage to the environment. As a result, xeriscaping not only reduces air, water, and soil pollution but also saves a lot of money.

The Seven Principles of Xeriscaping

1. **Planning and design:** *Planning and design* is key to having a good landscape and garden. The plan should show the major elements of the current landscape, including the view, soil, slopes, and direction of fences, walls, and existing trees, plants, and shrubs. Xeriscape landscapes should be divided into different zones with different water requirements. Wastewater or recycled water should be used for irrigating the landscape. This will reduce the demand for high amounts of water. Group plants according to their water and light requirements.

2. **Soil improvements:** *Soil* is the most important factor in xeriscape landscaping. If the soil is treated well, then it will in turn take good care of the plants. Xeriscape soil should provide ample nutrients and water to the plants; otherwise, the plants will weaken. Soil can be improved by increasing the amount of organic matter. This can increase the ability of the soil to absorb and store more water and nutrients. Soil also can be improved by using compost, peat moss, and careful use of fertilizers and pesticides.

3. **Efficient irrigation:** *Efficient irrigation* means proper utilization of water. Not all plants require the same amount of water. Group plants according to their water requirements. In xeriscape landscaping, plants do not need daily watering. Watering once a week is sufficient if the water is applied deep into

the roots. It is best to water infrequently and deeply to develop deep roots. Irrigation depends at which rate the water can be absorbed by the soil. Watering plants is not required frequently in spring and early summer.

4. **Mulch**: *Mulching* is necessary for xeriscape landscaping. It helps in improving the visual look of the garden. Mulching prevents erosion and weed growth. It also helps reduce evaporation and thus reduces the amount of water needed. Mulch also decomposes and feeds the soil. There are two types of mulching—*organic* and *inorganic*. Organic mulch is wood based and includes pole peelings, chipper chips, cedar chips, and decorative bark. Inorganic mulch is stone based and includes river rock, cobblestone, lava rock, and pea gravel.

5. **Maintenance**: Xeriscape landscaping requires *low maintenance*. A well-designed landscape can decrease the need for maintenance. Xeriscape landscapes need proper watering, weeding, pruning, fertilizing, and pest management. Mulching can reduce the growth of weeds. This will preserve and enhance the quality of the xeriscape.

6. **Appropriate plants**: Choosing *native plants* with minimal water needs will conserve the most water. Use drought-resistant plants, because their thick, small leaves help them save water. Group plants according to their water requirements.

7. **Turf areas**: *Turf grasses* are easy to maintain. They prevent erosion and are important for cooling the environment. Turf grasses also provide a play area for children. The location and selection of turf should be on the same basis as for the other plants, shrubs, and trees.

Benefits of Xeriscaping

- Water conservation
- Saves landfill space
- Low maintenance
- Minimal or no use of pesticides
- Reduces disease problems
- Provides a lot of attractive planting options
- Pollution free
- Raises property values
- Provides habitat for wildlife
- Reduces maintenance and water costs

Saving Water in Public Places

A *public place* is any area or establishment to which the public has access. Shops, schools, restaurants, hotels, parks, theaters, and clubs are examples of public places. People can visit a public place as a matter of right or by invitation. Some European countries, such as Norway, Sweden, and Finland, consider all nature areas public places.

Ways of Saving Water in Hotels and Restaurants

- Install signs and symbols of water conservation in customer restrooms.
- Increase employee awareness of water conservation.
- Offer suggestion boxes or seek suggestions from visitors on water conservation.
- Assign an employee to monitor water management.
- Determine the quantity of water used in various sections such as kitchens and bathrooms.
- Serve drinking water only when requested by customers.
- Immediately repair dripping faucets and showers to stop leakage.
- Use wastewater from bathtubs and sinks to flush toilets.
- Clean window glass only when required.
- Install flow reducers or adjusting devices in toilets.

Ways of Saving Water in Commercial Buildings

- Create employee awareness about saving water.
- Install water-saving signs inside office buildings and employee restrooms.

- Determine the amount of water to be used for various purposes.
- Assign an employee to monitor the using and saving of water.
- Install suggestion boxes and seek suggestions from employees and visitors.
- Shut the air conditioning off when it is not required.

Ways of Saving Water in Schools and Colleges

- Increase awareness among students about the importance of saving water.
- Make water conservation a part of the curriculum.
- Put water-conservation signs in the classrooms.
- Check the water supply system often, and repair any leaks.
- Sweep the floors more often than mopping.
- Use vacuum flush devices in toilet tanks.

Ways of Saving Water in Parks

- Use water for landscaping and gardening only when required.
- Watering two to three times a week is sufficient.
- Water in the early mornings or evenings to reduce evaporation.
- Use timers in sprinkler systems.
- Cover swimming pools when not in use to reduce evaporation.

Did you know?

About 95% of the 80 million people added to the world every year come from developing countries stressing the world's water supply.

Reclaimed/Graywater

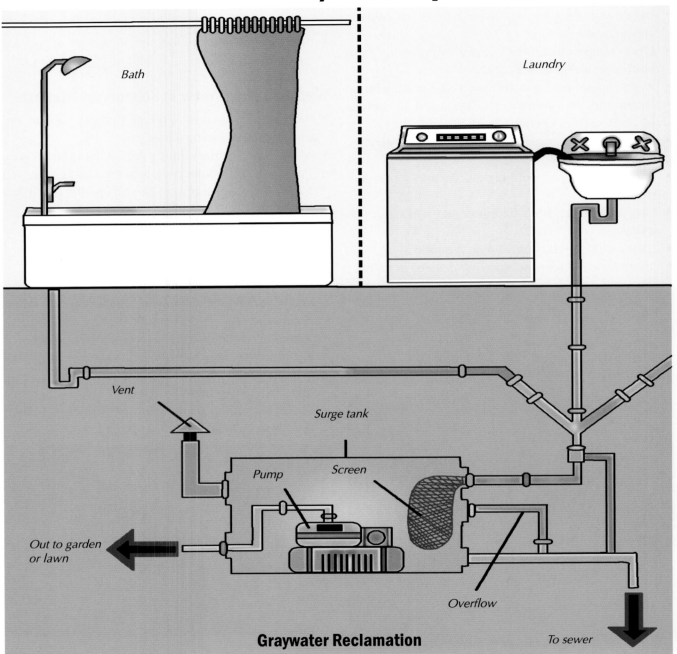

Bath

Laundry

Vent

Surge tank

Pump

Screen

Out to garden
or lawn

Overflow

Graywater Reclamation

To sewer

ousehold wastewater that can be reused for other purposes is known as *graywater*. It comes from sinks, showers, and baths but does not include toilet water. Treated graywater is known as *reclaimed water*.

Sources

Sources of graywater include the bathroom, kitchen, and laundry. Graywater comes from bathtubs, showers, washing machines, bathroom sinks, and laundry tubs. Wastewater from toilets and kitchen sinks or dishwashers is not considered graywater.

Ways to Use Graywater

- To irrigate ornamental plants, lawns, and trees other than food plants
- To make decorative fountains and ponds
- To sprinkle on dust on public roads
- To water golf courses
- To flush toilets

Did you know?

About 75% of the total wastewater that flows to domestic sewers is graywater.

Dos

- Filter graywater to separate hair and fiber particles from clothes.
- Check your garden often for any damage from organic materials in graywater.
- Use organic shampoos, detergents, and cleaning products that will not make graywater toxic and harm plants.
- If graywater has a high detergent concentration, it should be diluted with water.
- Rotate graywater irrigation with rainwater or potable water to reduce accumulation of salts in soil.

Don'ts

- Don't use graywater for drinking purposes.
- Don't use graywater where irrigation is done by spraying.
- Don't use graywater to irrigate root or leaf crops such as carrots, beets, and lettuce.
- Use of graywater is prohibited if any family members suffer from infectious diseases such as diarrhea and hepatitis.
- Don't allow graywater to leeach into ponds.
- Never use graywater from washed clothes spoiled by feces or vomit.
- Don't store untreated graywater for more than 24 hours. The bacteria in graywater will make it septic and could produce an offensive smell.
- Don't use graywater that contains harsh chemicals or bleaches that can kill beneficial soil organisms and damage plants.
- Don't wash your hands with graywater before eating or drinking.

Continuous
guttering

Rainwater
filter

Rainwater
storage
tank

Rainwater Collection

Rainwater Harvesting

Collecting water from rain and storing it for later use is known as *rainwater harvesting*. In this type of water conservation technique, rainwater is stored in tanks to be used later for domestic or agricultural purposes. Rainwater is also used to recharge groundwater so that it can be drawn when required.

Ancient Technique

Conserving water through rainwater harvesting is as old as human civilization. Rainwater was harvested more than 4,000 years ago in ancient Palestine and Greece. In the year 3000 BCE, the people of Baluchistan and Kutch irrigated crops by harvesting rainwater. The ancient Romans also built their homes in such a way to capture rainwater.

Applications of Rainwater Harvesting

Harvesting water from rain is useful for many purposes. Rainwater can be utilized for potable as well as nonpotable requirements. Potable uses of rainwater include drinking, cooking, bathing, and livestock feeding. Nonpotable uses include swimming pool replenishment, toilet flushing, laundry, and garden irrigation.

Did you know?

About 50% of domestic water consumption could come from rainwater harvesting.

Advantages of Rainwater Harvesting

- Rainwater is pure.
- It reduces strain on water supplies from other sources.
- Rainwater contains very little salt; it does not cause salt to accumulate in the soil.
- Rainwater harvesting helps reduce topsoil erosion.
- Rainwater is free of cost and thus lowers the water bill.
- In cities, rainwater harvesting reduces urban flooding.
- Rainwater harvesting is very useful in areas where floods occur frequently.
- Rainwater harvesting helps improve the groundwater level.
- Rainwater harvesting is most useful where groundwater is scarce or contaminated.
- Rainwater is free from pesticides, chlorine, and other manmade contaminants.

Countries Using Rainwater Harvesting

- Australia
- New Zealand
- Singapore
- India
- Germany
- China

Lakes and Depressions

Lakes and depressions are landforms on Earth's surface. *Lakes* are large bodies of water surrounded by land. Lakes are larger and deeper than ponds but smaller than a sea. Large lakes are often called seas. The world's largest lake is called the Caspian Sea. Most lakes are freshwater reservoirs. However, salty lakes are found in dry areas where water evaporates very quickly. Lakes such as the Caspian Sea, the Dead Sea, and Utah's Great Salt Lake are salty lakes.

Where are lakes found?

Most lakes on Earth are found in the Northern Hemisphere. North America has the highest number of lakes of any continent. In North America, Canada alone has about 50% of all lakes in the world. There are glacial lakes on the mountains of Europe, which are known as *tarns*.

Important Lakes

Some important lakes found on Earth are:

- Caspian Sea, Asia
- Aral Sea, Uzbekistan and Kazakhstan
- Baikal Lake, Russia
- Lake Tanganyika, Africa
- Lake Superior, United States and Canada
- Lake Michigan, United States
- Lake Erie, United States and Canada
- Lake Ontario, United States and Canada
- Lake Huron, United States and Canada
- Lake Titicaca, Bolivia and Peru
- Great Bear Lake, Canada

Caspian Sea

Ways of Increasing Lakes' Storage Capacity

Lakes store a large amount of fresh water. Lakes provide water for many important activities such as electricity generation, irrigation, and navigation. Excessive use of lake water shrinks lakes and sometimes even makes them go dry. For example, Utah's Great Salt Lake was much larger thousands of years ago. To make a lake more active and sustainable, its storage capacity needs to be increased. Some ways for improving a lake's water storage:

- Remove silt from the lake during the dry season with the help of dragline machines.
- Create proper channels so stormwater goes into the lake.
- Stop the inflow of sewage and wastewater from outside areas.
- Avoid taking baths, washing clothes, and cleaning vehicles near lakes.
- Plant trees near lakes to prevent soil erosion.

Did you know?

Earth's lakes and streams contain about 52,998 cubic miles of water.

Ways of Improving Water Quality

Lakes are important sources of drinking water. For safe drinking water, the quality of water has to be improved. Water quality can be improved by introducing aquatic plants and harvesting fish. Fish control aquatic weeds by feeding on them. By controlling weeds, fish help to keep the water clean and make it fit for drinking.

Floodplain Reservoirs

A *floodplain* is a frequently flooded land near rivers and streams. It is naturally flooded when rivers or streams overflow during the rainy seasons. A floodplain is formed naturally by the sediment deposited by rivers or lakes. Floodplains can be used to store water for later use. The stored water in a floodplain reservoir can be used for several purposes, such as to irrigate fields and to produce hydroelectric power. Through effective use of floodplains, we can conserve a huge amount of runoff water. Floodplain reservoirs help reduce water crises. The floodplains refresh groundwater and filter it every year.

Floodway

A *floodway* is the central portion of a floodplain. It is a section that represents the lowest point in a floodplain. It is also the most dangerous and risky part of a floodplain, because it has the deepest and fastest floodwaters. It is better to allow water to pass through a floodway without any obstruction. If floodwater is blocked in the floodway, then it may increase the water level and could become dangerous to human life.

Yamuna Floodplain

The *Yamuna floodplain* is located in Delhi, India, and covers an area of about 37.5 square miles. Delhi is facing the problem of increased need for fresh water because of growing population. The Yamuna floodplain stores monsoon water that is used later for most of the drinking water needs of Delhi. Floodplains provide a good option for providing clean drinking water.

Flood Fringe

The *flood fringe* is the outer section of the floodway. It has standing water instead of flowing water. A flood fringe has slow water flow and less severe depths than a floodway.

Floodplain Benefits

- Provides fertile agricultural land
- Recreational resource
- Provides habitat for wildlife and plants

Flora and Fauna of Floodplains

Plants

- Cattails
- Tamarack trees
- Water lilies

Amphibians

- Frogs and salamanders

Birds

- Canadian geese
- Cardinals
- Cranes
- Ducks

- Great blue herons
- Osprey
- Egrets
- Owls
- Redtailed hawks
- Trumpeter swans
- Blackbirds

Insects

- Dragonflies
- Mosquitoes
- Whirligig beetles

- Waterboatmen
- Monarch butterflies

Mammals

- Bats
- Beavers
- Raccoons
- River otters
- Mink

Reptiles

- Turtles

Quarry Reservoirs

Large, natural water-storage tanks known as *quarry* reservoirs are often formed in rock quarries. A *quarry* is a shallow, open pit left after the extraction of rocks or minerals. Quarry reservoirs are deep and have the capacity to store lots of water. Attached to water channels and rivers, they store excess water and decrease the possibility of flooding. Quarry reservoirs can be of any size or shape.

Types of Quarry Reservoirs

- Limestone
- Marble
- Sandstone
- Slate
- Granite
- Shale
- Clay

Benefits of a Quarry Reservoir

- Controls flooding
- Serves as water storage
- Available for use as an emergency water supply
- Helps the environment
- Encourages watershed protection
- Promotes water conservation
- Improves water quality
- Reduces water pollution
- Provides drinking water

Stone Quarry Reservoir

One quarry reservoir, called Stone Quarry Reservoir, is located in Carrboro, North Carolina. It was formerly a stone quarry used to extract stone for construction. It can store up to 200 million gallons of water.

By 2030, another much larger stone quarry will be ready for use in the area. It can store three billion gallons of water. It supplies water to the Carrboro-Chapel Hill community in North Carolina. It will raise water levels of nearby University Lake and the Cane Creek Reservoir. This will improve the region's environmental health and provide recreational opportunities. It will have other benefits as well.

Island Quarry Reservoir

The Island Quarry Reservoir is located at Byron Bay, New South Wales, Australia. It was formerly a quarry that excavated blue stone used for walkways and patios. Abandoned in 1980, it is spread over an eight-acre area. Today Island Quarry Reservoir is used mainly for recreation and tourism. It has become an arts and culture hub.

The Thornton Quarry Reservoir

The Thornton Quarry Reservoir is located in Illinois. It was formerly one of the world's largest limestone quarries. Now it serves as a reservoir to store sewer water during periods of heavy rainfall.

Crabtree Quarry

The Crabtree Quarry is located near Raleigh, North Carolina. Situated near Crabtree Creek, it was formerly a quarry where crystals were mined. Every year Crabtree Creek overflows due to heavy rainfall and causes problems for homes and businesses. The Crabtree Quarry stores extra water and reduces the possibility of floods. Water stored for long periods settles sediment, thus improving water quality.

Calero Dam and Reservoir

Calero Dam and Reservoir, located in Santa Clara, California, is built on Calero Creek. *Calero* is a Spanish term that means "limestone quarry." This reservoir covers an area of 349 acres and the capacity to store 9,934 acre-feet of water.

Almaden Dam and Reservoir

Almaden Dam and Reservoir is also located in Santa Clara, California. In Spanish, *almaden* means "mineral" or "mine." Mercury was formerly mined there, and at one time Almaden Reservoir was considered the largest store of water in America. The reservoir covers an area of 57 acres and has the capacity to store 1,586 acre-feet of water.

Spring Creek Reservoir

Spring Creek Reservoir is another water storage area in Santa Clara. It was formerly a stone quarry and was abandoned in 1987. Now it is used to control floods. It stores extra floodwater from Springbrook Creek.

Did you know?

At least 50% of the world's wetlands have been destroyed. As a result, more than 20% of the world's freshwater animal and plant species have already become extinct.

Ancient Reservoirs

The oldest manmade structures on Earth for storing water are known as *ancient reservoirs*. These include dams, ponds, lakes, and wells. They have been around since the earliest human civilizations of Egypt and Mesopotamia. The Jawa Dam in Jordan was built by the Mesopotamians around 3000 BCE. Ancient reservoirs were built primarily to provide water for irrigation. Later, people started using them for domestic water supplies. The reservoirs also helped by providing water in droughts. In early times, travelers and soldiers were largely dependent on them for water. This is why most of the ancient reservoirs are located on military and trade routes.

Unearthing Ancient Reservoirs

- Many ancient reservoirs are buried at a depth of about 90 to 150 feet underground. These have to be uncovered by removing the soil.
- Most ancient reservoirs are located near or linked with rivers, which helps in recharging water by making proper incoming channels.

Some Famous Ancient Reservoirs

- Kosheis Reservoir (2900 BCE) in Egypt
- Moeris Reservoir (2300 BCE) in Egypt
- Basawakkulam Reservoir (430 BCE) in Sri Lanka
- Girnar Reservoir (300 BCE) in India
- Cornalbo and Proserpina Reservoirs (100 CE) in Spain

Some Ancient Reservoirs

- The Romans were very good users of water. Around the first century CE, they constructed many dams near the Mediterranean Sea to hold water from rivers. The largest reservoir made by the Romans is Lake Homs, which is now in Syria. It was created in 284 CE, and it could hold nearly 90 million cubic yards of water.

- A *baoli* is a kind of ancient reservoir found in northern India. Baolis are step-wells used to collect and store rainwater. Most of the baolis are found in Delhi. Constructed in the 10th century, Anangtal is the oldest existing baoli in Delhi. Baolis were also places of social gathering at that time.

- Most of the ancient temples in southern India have large tanks on their premises. These tanks are fed either by rainwater or by underground springs. The areas of these tanks vary from about one to seven acres. They supplied drinking water and also fulfilled religious purposes.

Advantages of Ancient Reservoirs

- Ancient reservoirs have sand and gravel layers that increase the storage capacity.
- Ancient reservoirs have ideal rock strata for storage. These are porous rocks from which extra groundwater can be extracted.
- Ancient reservoirs are a relatively good source of recharging groundwater, as they commonly serve as flood channels or aqueducts.
- Ancient reservoirs have good filtration, as their surface is usually made up of sandy soil.

Did you know?

The earliest ancient reservoirs were dams. Marib Dam in Yemen (constructed more than 2,700 years ago) was built by the Mesopotamian civilization.

Paleo-Channels

Old abandoned river courses are known as *paleo-channels*. Paleo is a Greek term meaning "ancient or something old." They are also known as paleo drainage, lost rivers, buried rivers, buried channels, or buried valleys. A long time ago, paleo-channels were active rivers or streams, but natural or manmade disasters made them dry up. Some also became dry due to changes in river flow. Paleo-channels have good underground water storage. They store water just a few yards beneath the ground. Paleo-channels can be of linear, zigzag, or many other shapes.

Paleo-Channels as a Recharge Location

Paleo-channels' structure is ideal for water storage. They include various kinds of rock with differing water-storage qualities. This variation helps people in various geographical locations use them during floods or for rainwater harvesting. Most paleo-channels are interlinked with existing rivers, creeks, or channels.

Paleo-Channels as Aquifers

Due to geographical or climatic disasters, paleo-channels were long ago buried or shifted to other places. They are a rich source of aquifers and can help meet the decreasing water supply. With the help of satellites, geologists try to locate paleo-channels. During floods or heavy rainfall, water can be turned toward these abandoned channels. This helps in using water from aquifers that were left abandoned.

Advantages of Paleo-Channels

- They provide information to geologists about different water-storage locations.
- They provide information about rivers of past times.
- They provide information about different climatic changes that happened in the past.
- They can help geologists predict future climate shifts.
- In coastal regions, paleo-channels can provide a hydraulic connection between freshwater aquifers and the sea, making it easier to bring saltwater inland or take fresh water out to sea.
- They often contain deposits of valuable minerals like tin, tungsten, gold, silver, and diamonds.

Types of Paleo-Channels

According to their landform characteristics, paleo-channels can be divided into four categories:
- Upland paleo-channel belts
- Strip-shaped upland paleo-channels
- Trough-shaped depression paleo-channels
- Ancient riverbeds

Check Dams

Small dams called *check dams* are sometimes built on small rivers and streams for harvesting water. Check dams collect rainwater during monsoons and help to refill the groundwater level. Check dams are very effective because they store water for use both during and after the monsoon. They store water for future use during the dry season, for irrigation, for livestock, and for domestic needs. Check dams can be constructed at a low cost from easily available materials such as rock, gravel, sandbags, fiber rolls, and even recycled products.

Types of Check Dams

Rock Check Dams

Rock check dams are small dams constructed across a drainage way. They usually are constructed from large rocks about 8 to 12 inches in diameter. Rock check dams have proven to be an efficient way to control soil erosion. They are more stable and rarely slip or slide from their position.

Log Check Dams

Log check dams are temporary dams constructed from logs. The logs used to build a check dam should be about 4 to 6 inches in diameter and are fixed into the soil. Log check dams are constructed within a channel or ditch or across a drainage way. The purpose of a log check dam is the same as that of rock check dams: to prevent soil erosion. They also help in slowing down the speed of flowing water, thus allowing sediment to settle.

Sandbag Check Dams

Sandbag check dams are small, temporary check dams. The sandbags are filled with sand and constructed across a drainage way, ditch, or channel. These check dams are easy to construct and require low maintenance.

Maintenance of Check Dams

Check dams should be inspected regularly. They need to be checked after every rainfall. If there is any damage, such as stones having been washed downstream, the dam should be repaired immediately. Accumulated sediment behind the dam should also be removed when necessary.

Advantages of Check Dams

- Inexpensive to construct
- Easy to build
- Prevent soil erosion
- No acquisition of land required
- Accessible to poor farmers
- Low maintenance
- Increase soil moisture and vegetation
- Reduce damage from flash floods
- Effective method of water conservation
- Provide employment
- Easy availability of drinking water

Disadvantages of Check Dams

- Installation and removal of check dams can damage vegetation
- Used only in small open channels
- May kill grass lining in channels
- Require high maintenance during high-velocity flows
- Not used in live channels or streams

Did you know?

The United States has more than 2.5 million dams.

Village Ponds

Manmade water reservoirs known as *village ponds* are the primary source of drinking water for people living in villages. Village ponds are also used for bathing, washing clothes, and providing drinking water for cattle. They are used to irrigate crops by supplying water to adjacent irrigation wells. Village ponds are found in most parts of the world.

How to Increase Storage Capacity of Ponds

- Deepen the pond by removing silt with the help of dragline machines.
- Garbage dumping must be avoided.
- Plant grasses along the sloping perimeter of the pond to reduce soil erosion.
- Make proper channels to let stormwater run into the village pond.
- Ponds can be connected with rivers and deep trenches to increase storage during flood season.
- Remove unnecessary vegetation, roots, and organic matter from the pond.
- Build structures such as *weirs* (also known as *lowhead dams*) at the inlet so inflowing rainwater or floodwater does not cause gully erosion.

Duckweed

Improving Water Quality of Ponds

- Keep sewage diverted away from the village pond.
- Control harvesting of fish, as they act as a purifier, feeding on mosquito larvae and aquatic plants.
- Introduce aquatic plants such as duckweed, which can accumulate nutrients and toxic elements in water and keep them from polluting water. Duckweed is also a rich food source for fish.
- Introduce beneficial pond bacteria, which is an organic way to keep pond water clean. Bacteria consume organic wastes that otherwise would decompose and release toxins such as ammonia and nitrite into the water. These bacteria also reduce odors in pond water.
- Cover the embankment with topsoil and plant quick-growing grasses. Do not plant trees on the embankment.

Grasses planted along the perimeter of a pond

Did you know?

Most people in developing countries walk at least three hours to fetch water.

Ecoparks

Artificial wetlands known as *ecoparks* are manmade areas built to treat water. They are also known as *artificial wetlands* because they are designed, built, and operated by humans. Ecoparks are similar to natural wetlands but within a more controlled environment. They are complex systems in which water, wildlife, microorganisms, and the environment interact with each other to treat the wastewater. The primary purpose of a wetland is to treat or improve the quality of water. Artificial wetlands also provide a habitat for animals and plants. These wetlands are an efficient way to remove pollutants from municipal and industrial wastewater.

What are wetlands?

Wetlands are areas that are covered by water, either seasonally or permanently. They occur where the land is covered by shallow water. Wetlands are also known as *swamps, marshes, bogs, fens, wet meadows, sloughs,* or, in some parts of the United States, *cienegas* and *tinajas.* Wetlands are an important type of ecosystem and are commonly found throughout the world. They are home to many species of plants and animals not found elsewhere. About 6% of Earth's land surface is made up of wetlands, covering around 2.2 million square miles.

Why make artificial wetlands?

Artificial wetlands are created to treat or improve the quality of wastewater. They are an effective way to remove pollutants from contaminated water. Artificial wetlands are easy to construct and less expensive in comparison to conventional sewage treatment plants. Artificial wetlands can treat water from various sources including domestic, agricultural, industrial, and mining wastewaters. They provide a good alternative for wastewater treatment facilities and allow reuse and recycling of water. Artificial wetlands also attract wildlife and provide opportunities for environmental educators.

Types of Artificial Wetlands

Subsurface Flow Systems

Subsurface flow systems are designed with underground water flowing through a sand or gravel bed. They consist of a sealed basin with a porous substrate of rock or gravel. Root systems penetrate to the bottom of the bed. These are also known as *root-zone systems, rock-reed filters,* or *vegetated submerged beds*. They prevent odors and other problems.

Surface Flow Systems

Surface flow systems are designed with water flowing above ground. These systems are usually designed for treating municipal water. Surface flow systems consist of a shallow basin with soil or other medium to support the roots. They are often known as *free-water-surface wetlands*.

Vegetation

Artificial wetlands have both *vascular* and *nonvascular* plants. Vascular plants help treat wastewater. They absorb carbon and other substances and incorporate them into tiny plant tissues. Vascular plants help transfer gases between the atmosphere and the sediment. Microbes are attracted to stem and root systems of vascular plants. Vascular plants create litter when they die or decay. These plants slow down the flow of water, which further allows the materials to settle. During photosynthesis, algae increase the dissolved oxygen content of the water. Artificial wetlands are also planted with non-woody plants including bulrushes, cattails, reeds, and a number of broad-leaved species.

Advantages of Artificial Wetlands

- Less expensive than traditional sewage treatment
- Reduce water odors
- Treat different types of wastewater
- Provide effective water treatment
- Provide wildlife habitat
- Increase vegetation
- Reduce contaminants
- Low maintenance cost
- Allow water reuse and recycling
- Environment-friendly
- Require less or no energy
- Easy to construct

Disadvantages of Artificial Wetlands

- Require larger area
- Mosquitoes and other pests
- Unable to treat high concentration of certain pollutants
- Treatment dependent on climatic conditions

Constructed Wetlands Treat Water From Many Different Sources:

- Drainage water from mines
- Runoff from highways
- Agricultural wastewater (including livestock waste, runoff, and drainage water)
- Sewage (from small communities, individual homes, and businesses)
- Stormwater
- Water leached from landfills
- Partially treated industrial wastewater

Artificial Wetlands Differ From Natural Wetlands in the Following Ways:

- Constant in size
- Not connected directly to groundwater
- Hold greater amount of sediment
- Plants and organisms develop very fast

Did you know?

On Earth, freshwater animals are disappearing five times faster than land animals.

Water Contaminants

Elements that make water impure and unhealthy for drinking are known as *water contaminants*. Like air, water is found almost everywhere on Earth. Whenever water is exposed to contaminants, it becomes unfit for human consumption. We call it *dirty water*. There are different types of water contaminants. They can be living organisms, naturally occurring substances, or manmade synthetic compounds. These contaminants include medical wastes, asbestos, chlorine, mercury, nitrates, pesticides, and volatile organic compounds. Until now, more than 70,000 different water contaminants have been identified on Earth. Contaminated water has become a threat to human life.

Microbes

Microbes are biological contaminants. They are very tiny organisms. Microbes are so-called because they can be seen only with the help of a microscope. Organisms such as bacteria, fungi, viruses, parasites, and so on are called microbes. Microbes are also called *pathogens* as they can cause serious diseases. Microbes get into water through sewage and animal waste. Some water contaminant microbes are:

- *Fecal coliforms* and *E. coli* are bacteria that live in human and animal fecal waste. They contaminate water as it comes into contact with the waste. Fecal coliforms and *E. coli* can cause diarrhea, cramps, nausea, and headaches.
- *Cryptosporidium* is a parasite commonly found in lakes and rivers. It affects the body's immune systems.
- *Turbidity* is the contamination of water due to sediment from soil runoff. Water with high turbidity levels contains higher amounts of clay and silt. Turbidity harbors harmful bacteria and viruses and can cause nausea, cramps, diarrhea, and headaches.
- *Giardia lamblia* is a type of bacteria that contaminates lakes and river water and causes illnesses such as giardiasis (also known as *backpacker's diarrhea* or *beaver fever*), diarrhea, vomiting, and cramps.

Organic Contaminants

- *Benzene* is an organic liquid used for making paints, plastics, rubber, resins, and synthetic fabrics such as nylon and polyester. Benzene enters water from discharged factory wastes and contaminates water. Benzene can cause anemia, nervous system disorders, and even cancer.
- *Alachlor* is an herbicide used to control weeds in crops such as corn, sorghum, and soybeans. Alachlor can cause damage to the liver, kidneys, spleen, and nose and eyelid linings.
- *Acrylamide* is an organic solid used in drinking water treatment, to improve production from oil wells, in textile factories, and in construction of dams and tunnels. Acrylamide causes nervous system damage, paralysis, and cancer.
- MTBE (methyl tertiary-butyl ether) is a gasoline additive used to reduce vehicle emissions. MTBE comes into contact with water through motorboats, leaking gasoline tanks, pipelines, and spills. MTBE causes an odor and unpleasant taste in water.

Inorganic Contaminants

Inorganic contaminants are of mineral origin. Inorganic water contaminants include toxic metals such as arsenic, asbestos, lead, and mercury. These contaminants can get into drinking water from the release of industrial wastes into water, from materials used in plumbing systems, and from natural sources such as soil erosion.

- *Lead* is a metal that contaminates water from plumbing pipes. Lead delays physical and mental growth in children. In adults, it causes high blood pressure and damages the kidneys.
- *Asbestos* is a fibrous material used for roofing, cement pipes, brake pads, and many other purposes. Exposure to asbestos through drinking water can cause lung disease and cancer.
- *Mercury* is a liquid metal used in electrical equipment. Mercury gets into water from industrial waste and soil erosion. Mercury is very harmful to the kidneys and brain.
- *Arsenic* is a naturally occurring toxic metal used in gardens to kill weeds and pests. Arsenic contaminates water from garden runoff and glass factory wastes. Arsenic damages the skin, hampers the circulatory system, and can cause cancer.
- *Nitrate* is an inorganic contaminant that contaminates water through fertilizer runoff. Nitrate can cause "blue baby syndrome" in infants and shortness of breath.
- *Fluoride* is a mineral added to water to make strong teeth. It also comes from fertilizers and aluminum factories. Excessive fluoride in water can cause pain and tenderness of bones.

Radionuclide

Radionuclide water contaminants are radioactive elements that emit rays. A radioactive element decays continually and emits radiation in the form of alpha, beta, and gamma rays. Radionuclide contaminants such as radium and uranium occur naturally in soil and rocks. They also can be produced artificially.

Did you know?

Each day, about 500,000 tons of contaminants are released into the rivers and lakes in the United States.

Drinking Water Treatment

The process that makes water suitable for human consumption is known as *drinking water treatment*. Most of the water we find around us is *not* safe and clean. Water can be contaminated by many sources, including animal waste, agricultural chemicals, lawn and garden chemicals, and hazardous household wastes. Contaminated drinking water can cause diseases such as cholera, typhoid, and dysentery. Drinking water treatment helps to purify impure water and makes it useful for human consumption. It not only makes water clean and safe, but also removes odors and makes water taste better so it is suitable for household use. About 1.1 billion people, or 18% of the world's population, still don't have enough safe drinking water.

History of Drinking Water Treatment

The idea of drinking water treatment dates back to 4,000 BCE. Ancient Sanskrit and Greek literature mentioned various methods for treating water. In ancient times, people treated water to remove turbidity or "muddiness" in water. People used to treat water by boiling it, filtering it through charcoal, exposing it to sunlight, or straining it. By 1500 BCE, the Egyptians used the chemical *alum* to purify water. During the 18th century, two scientific discoveries made drinking water treatment popular in Europe. The first was Dr. John Snow's discovery of cholera as a waterborne disease in 1855, and the second was Louis Pasteur's "germ theory" in the late 1800s. Pasteur's theory explained that water contains many microscopic organisms that can transmit diseases to humans. In 1914, the U.S. Public Health Service set standards for drinking water treatment.

Boiling

Boiling is an easy drinking water treatment method. In boiling, water is put into a clean container and brought to a full boil for at least three minutes. Boiled water is normally covered and stored until it is ready to be used.

Advantages
- It is the best method in emergency conditions.
- It kills harmful bacteria and other living organisms like *Giardia lamblia* and *Cryptosporidium*, which are normally found in rivers and lakes.

Disadvantages
- It cannot remove toxic elements such as lead, mercury, and asbestos from water.
- It requires fuel and cooking equipment.
- Boiled water cannot be used immediately, as it needs to cool down.
- Particles may remain after boiling.

Distillation

In *distillation*, water is boiled in a chamber and allowed to evaporate. The vaporized water vapor is pure water, with all salts, sediment, and metallic contents removed. The water vapor is stored in another chamber and allowed to cool until it becomes liquid water.

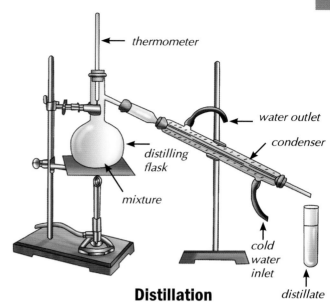

Distillation

Labels: thermometer, water outlet, condenser, distilling flask, mixture, cold water inlet, distillate

Advantages
- It produces very pure water.
- It can remove nitrates, chloride, and other salts.
- It also kills bacteria in water.

Disadvantages
- It is a time-consuming method and can take two to five hours to make about one gallon of distilled water.
- It requires electricity.
- It requires frequent cleaning of the devices.

Filtration

Filtration is a process where water passes through filters. It is the earliest drinking water treatment method. Filtration removes fine suspended solids from water.

Reverse Osmosis

Reverse osmosis is a very popular drinking water treatment process. In reverse osmosis, water is forced to pass through a membrane that has extremely tiny pores. The membrane allows water to pass through but keeps particles out. It is the best method when water contains high levels of dissolved contaminants.

Advantages
- It effectively reduces salt dissolved in water.
- It can remove very tiny organisms such as viruses.
- It is less expensive to operate and maintain.
- It does not require electricity.

Reverse Osmosis

Applied pressure

Pure water

Semipermeable membrane

Direction of pure water

Disadvantages

- It produces wastewater–about two to four gallons of wastewater are produced for each gallon of treated water.
- A damaged membrane cannot be detected easily, but once damaged, it cannot effectively purify water.
- This process requires high water pressure. In emergencies, when there is less water pressure, it may not work properly.

Ultraviolet Radiation

Drinking water can be treated with *ultraviolet radiation*. In this process, water is exposed to ultraviolet light. Ultraviolet light helps purify water by destroying bacteria and viruses.

Advantages

- It does not leave any taste or smell in the treated water.
- It takes less time.
- It does not affect mineral content in water.

Disadvantages

- It is not suitable for water contaminated with high levels of solids.

- It cannot remove toxic elements such as lead, asbestos, and chlorine.
- It requires electricity to operate.

Bottled Water

Bottled water is treated water that is sold in bottles. This water is thoroughly filtered, and then beneficial minerals are added back in to make it taste better.

Advantages

- It is a good emergency source of pure water.
- Bottled water is a safe and reliable source of drinking water outside the home.
- It tastes better, as it is chlorine-free.

Disadvantages

- Bottled water is costlier than water from other treatment processes.
- Producing bottles requires resources.
- Empty bottles cause a waste-disposal problem.

Desalination

Desalination is a process of making saltwater fresh and drinkable. In desalination, seawater is treated to remove salts and other impurities. Desalination is an extensive method that includes several other water treatment methods, such as reverse osmosis and distillation.

Did you know?

In the United States, about 48 million people get their drinking water from household wells.

Advantages

- It produces very safe and high-quality drinking water.
- It is useful in areas where fresh water is scarce.

Disadvantages

- The process is quite expensive and consumes a lot of energy.
- It produces waste, which needs to be disposed of properly.

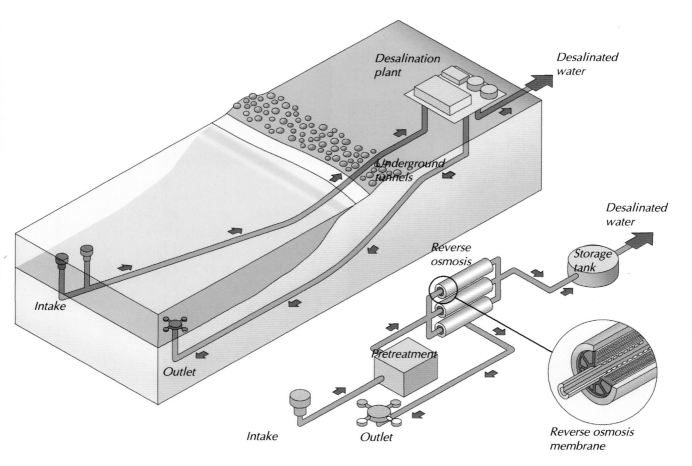

Desalination

Facts and Figures

1. The amount of water on Earth is about the same as it was millions of years ago.
2. Nearly 97% of the world's water is salty or otherwise undrinkable, 2% is locked in ice caps and glaciers, and only 1% is left for our needs.
3. The people of the United States drink a total of about 110 million gallons of water per day.
4. Nearly 100 gallons of water can be wasted through a leaky faucet in a day.
5. About 6.5 gallons of water is used for just one flush of the toilet.
6. An average family of four uses nearly 881 gallons of water per week just by flushing the toilet.
7. An average bath requires 37 gallons of water.
8. By repairing a leaky toilet, one can save more than 50 gallons of water per day.

9. The average American uses a total of about 140 to 170 gallons of water per day.
10. An American family of four uses up to 260 gallons of water per day in the home by:
    - Running tap for two minutes: three to five gallons
    - Flushing toilet once: five to seven gallons
    - Showering, five minutes: 20 to 35 gallons
    - Full bathtub: 60 gallons
    - Automatic dishwasher: 10 to 20 gallons
11. Showering and bathing consume the largest percentage of domestic water, which is about 27% of an average household's water.
12. If every household in the United States had a faucet that dripped once each second, 928 million gallons of water a day would leak away.

13. An automatic dishwasher uses 9 to 12 gallons of water, while hand-washing dishes can use up to 20 gallons.

14. Water lawns during the early morning hours, or in the evening when temperatures and wind speed are the lowest. This reduces losses from evaporation.

15. Approximately one million miles of pipelines and aqueducts carry water in the United States and Canada. That is enough pipes to circle Earth 40 times.

16. Some 300 million gallons of water is needed to produce a single day's supply of newsprint for U.S. newspapers.

17. Around the world, about 54% of the available fresh water is used in a year. This figure is expected to go up to 70% by 2025.

18. Water helps to regulate Earth's temperature.

Index

Glossary

agriculture: growing and raising of crops and animals for food

aquatic: ability to that live or grow in or on water

atmosphere: the layer of gases that surround the Earth

bacteria: microscopic, single-celled organisms that can cause diseases

climate: weather in a particular region over a long period

condense: to change from a vapor or gas to a liquid

conservation: protection or management of valuable resources, such as water

contaminate: to pollute by direct contact

decompose: to break down and decay

dissolve: to separate into molecules in a liquid

drought: a long period of little or no rain

ecosystem: a complex community of living things in a physical environment

erosion: wearing away of land or soil by water, wind, animals, and even human activity

evaporation: the process by which a liquid turns into gas

extinct: a species that no longer exists

fertilizer: a chemical substance used to improve the fertility of soil

glacier: a large body of ice that moves very slowly

global warming: an increase in the average temperature of the Earth

groundwater: fresh water found beneath the surface of the ground

habitat: an environment in which a plant or animal normally lives and grows

hemisphere: a half of the Earth on either side of the equator

indigenous: belonging naturally to a given region or ecosystem

irrigation: the addition of water to agricultural land using sprinklers, pumps, or pipes

migrate: move from one place to another to live, spawn or feed

monsoon: a seasonal wind that brings heavy rain and flooding during summer especially in southern Asia

nutrients: substances that help living things be healthy and grow

organism: any living structure—plant, animal, fungus, bacterium—that is capable of growth and reproduction

parasite: an animal that lives on or in another animal that and feeds on it

peat: marshy soil that is made up of decomposed plants

pest: animal or plant that causes harm to other animals or plants

pesticide: any chemical compound that is used to kill pests

pollutant: a substance that contaminates and pollutes air, water, and land

precipitation: falling products of condensation of water vapor in the atmosphere, as in rain, snow, or hail

radiation: rays or waves of energy emitted from the sun

reed: grass-like plants that grow in groups in shallow water

reservoir: a lake that is used to store water

resource: something ready to use

runoff: water that drains or flows off the land into streams and ditches

sediment: small particles such as sand or gravel that settles on land or on ocean floor

topsoil: fertile, upper layer of soil that contains the nutrients needed by plants to grow well

toxin: poisonous substances caused by pollution

treat: to apply special substances to give a particular quality

urban: related to city or town

vapor: the gaseous form of something that is usually liquid

volatile organic compound (VOC): a carbon-rich chemical that evaporates at room temperature

wetland: land such as swamp or marsh